The Creatures of Imagination

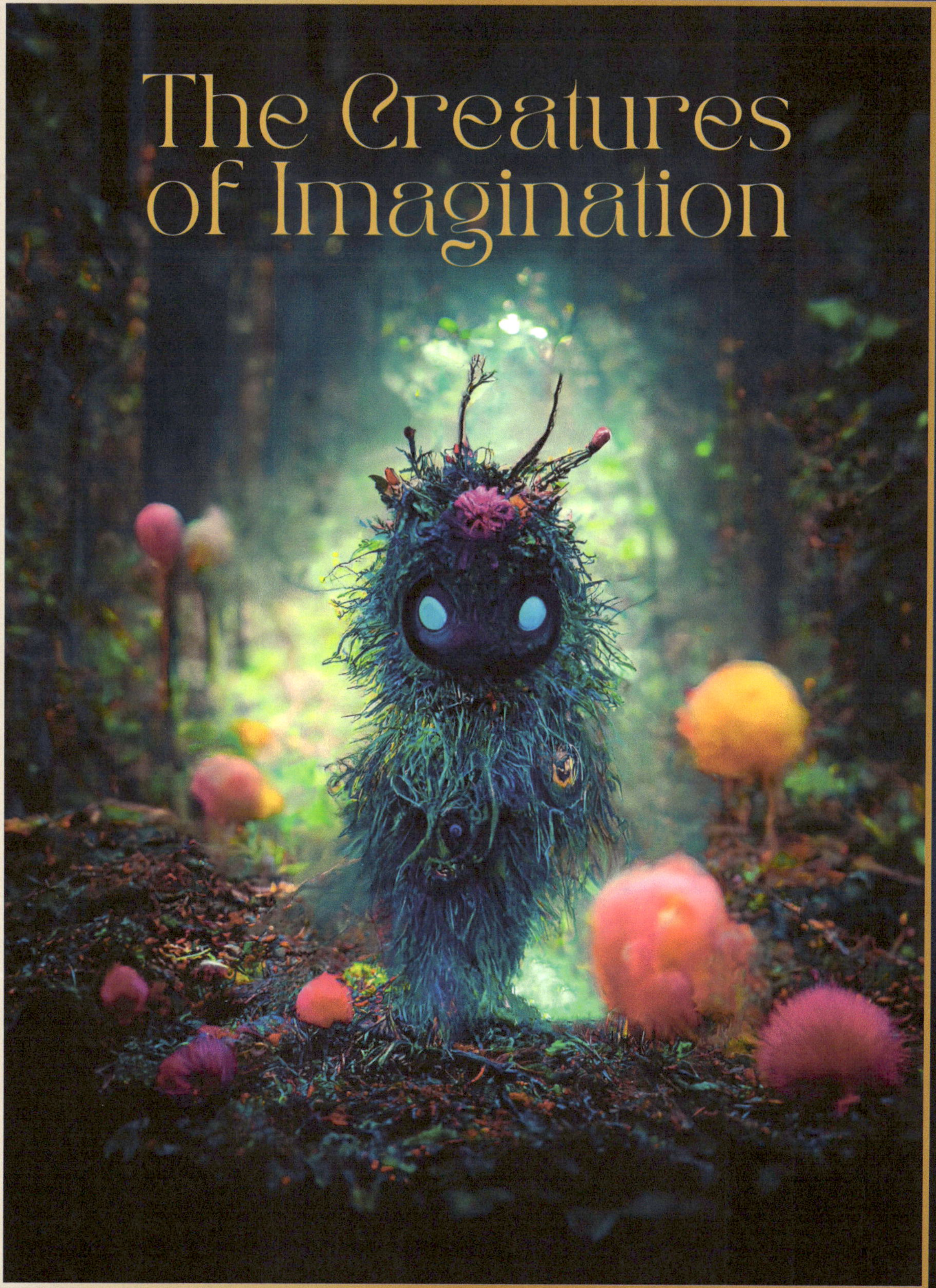

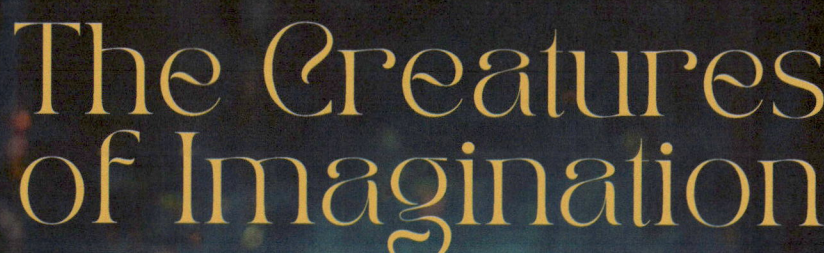

First published in 2022
Written and Illustrated by Amber Cox
Book design by Bryony van der Merwe

ISBN: 979-8-218-05680-3

All Creatures of Imagination
were brought to life
with the magic of AI.

The Creatures of Imagination
from the Valley of Inspiration...

A perfect land where creatures
of all shapes and sizes
can roam free.

The Valley of Inspiration really
is the most magical place to be!

They are always
creating new things
and sharing them
with their friends.

And sharing exciting stories
with beginnings,
middles, and ends!

The creatures of the Valley
know that everything
can be achieved

All you have to do
is put your mind to it
and truly believe!

The Creatures of Imagination
are all around us –
Up and down
and left and right

So no matter what
happens each day,
the future is always bright!

Anything is possible,
as long as you
truly believe!

Did you like this book?

Please take a moment
to leave a review on
Amazon.